Cinderella's Wedding

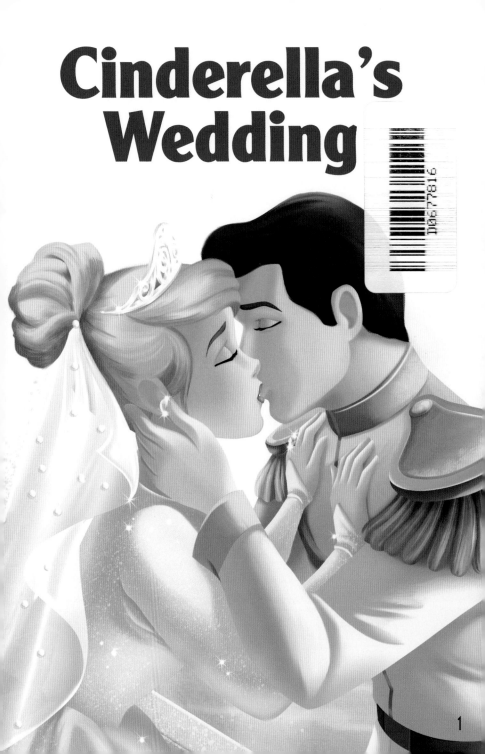

Here is the dress.
The dress is ready.

Here is the feast.
The feast is ready.

Here are the guests.
The guests are ready.

Here are the rings.
The rings are ready.

Here is Cinderella.
Cinderella is ready.

Cinderella and the Prince are married!

What about the cake?
The cake is ready, too. Yum!